The Neighbor She Never Knew

By

AURELIE DUNCANSON

ACKNOWLEDGEMENT

To my family, for your endless love and encouragement, you've been my greatest strength.

To my friends, who cheered me on even in moments of doubt.

To the incredible editors and mentors whose guidance shaped this story into what it is.

To my readers, you're the heart of every word written here.

And to every inspiration along the way, thank you for making this adventure possible.

TABLE OF CONTENTS

CHAPTER 1

THE PERFECT MOVE-IN

Moving day on Cypress Avenue was usually an event. Neighbors peeked through their curtains, speculating about the new arrivals, debating whether they'd fit the pristine mold of our quiet Monterey suburb but that morning, as I stood on my porch with my coffee, watching the large moving truck roll to a stop across the street, I sensed that this time was different.

The new house had sat empty for months, its windows staring blankly at the rest of the neighborhood, waiting for life to return inside. Kate had walked past it countless times, always wondering why no one moved in, who had lived there before - if anyone at all. Now, movers filed in and out, carrying boxes stamped with neatly printed labels. Expensive furniture wrapped in plastic followed, hinting that whoever was moving in wasn't just another average family.

And then, she appeared.

A slender woman stepped onto the porch, her auburn hair catching the sunlight in waves. She carried herself with the kind of elegance that wasn't forced but ingrained—like she belonged anywhere she went. Her icy blue eyes scanned the street, landing on me briefly before she offered a small, polite smile. She didn't wave. She didn't look uncertain or overwhelmed, the way most new neighbors did.

She looked perfect.

There was something about her, something effortless yet... calculated. I couldn't explain it, but the pull was immediate. The kind that makes you want to walk up and introduce yourself before you even think about why.

And that's exactly what I did.

"Welcome to the neighborhood," I called out, stepping across the freshly cut grass that separated our houses. I kept my voice light, friendly, but I couldn't deny the curiosity creeping in. It wasn't every day that someone new moved onto Cypress Avenue, and certainly not someone who looked like her—delicate, sophisticated, like she belonged somewhere else entirely.

She turned toward me, her icy blue eyes locking onto mine with an intensity that was almost unsettling. But then she smiled, and the moment passed.

"Thank you," she said warmly. Her voice was smooth, practiced. "I'm Isabella. My husband, Steven, and I just moved in." She gestured vaguely toward the house, but there was no sign of this supposed husband.

I glanced at the movers, wondering if one of them might be Steven, but they all seemed too busy with their work to belong to the perfectly put-together woman in front of me.

"I'm Kate. My husband, Liam, and I live right next door." I extended a hand, and she took it, her grip cool and measured. "It's a great neighborhood—quiet, safe. You'll love it here."

"That's what we were hoping for," she said, her gaze drifting toward the tree-lined street. The words sounded genuine enough, but something about the way she said we felt off.

Before I could dwell on it, she continued, "Steven's away for business, unfortunately. He travels a lot." She sighed, tucking a loose strand of hair behind her ear. "I'm still getting used to being alone in a new city."

There it was—that perfect blend of vulnerability and charm. She wasn't just a beautiful woman moving into the neighborhood; she was a lonely beautiful woman. And whether she meant to or not, she had just pulled me in.

"Well, if you ever need anything, I'm right next door," I offered, ignoring the slight tug of unease in my stomach. "We could grab coffee sometime?"

Her smile widened, just enough to seem grateful, just enough to make me feel like I had done something good. "I'd love that."

***

Later that evening, as I was setting the table for dinner, Liam walked in, rolling up the sleeves of his button-down. His hazel eyes flickered toward the window facing Isabella's house.

"Made a new friend?" he asked, grabbing a glass of water.

I shrugged. "She seems nice."

"Or she seems too nice." His voice carried that familiar note of caution, the one I had learned to recognize as his Kate, don't get too involved tone.

I sighed, placing the plates down with a little more force than necessary. "What's that supposed to mean?"

He leaned against the counter, taking a sip of water. "It means you have a habit of getting curious about people. And curiosity usually turns into something else."

I crossed my arms. "You make it sound like I'm some conspiracy theorist."

"You are a conspiracy theorist," he deadpanned.

I rolled my eyes. "I'm just being neighborly. She's new, and she doesn't know anyone. What was I supposed to do? Ignore her?"

Liam sighed, setting his glass down. "Look, all I'm saying is, maybe let her settle in before you start playing detective."

I waved him off, but a part of me knew he was right. I did have a tendency to get involved. But this wasn't one of those times. Isabella was just another new neighbor, and I was just being polite.

At least, that's what I told myself.

***

The next morning, I found Isabella sitting on her porch, a steaming cup of coffee cradled between her hands. Even in a simple knit sweater and leggings, she looked effortlessly elegant, as if the chilly morning air had been designed to complement her presence rather than disturb it.

"Mind if I join you?" I called out.

She looked up, startled at first, then offered a slow, easy smile. "Not at all."

I settled into the chair beside her, tucking my legs beneath me as I wrapped my hands around my own coffee mug. The crisp air carried the scent of damp leaves and fresh earth—a reminder that autumn was creeping in.

"Settling in okay?" I asked.

She exhaled, her breath curling in the cool air. "Trying to. Everything still feels a little… foreign."

I nodded. "Yeah, moving can be overwhelming. You'll get used to it."

She glanced toward the street, watching the occasional passing car. "It's so quiet here," she mused. "Almost too quiet."

I chuckled. "Trust me, you'll appreciate that soon enough. No late-night sirens, no neighbors blasting music at two in the morning. It's peaceful."

She tilted her head slightly. "But doesn't it ever feel… isolating?"

I hesitated. It wasn't something I had thought about before, at least not in those words. "I guess that depends," I said carefully. "Some people like having space. Others need constant noise."

"Which one are you?" she asked, turning her gaze on me.

The way she looked at me then—intensely, like she was dissecting my answer before I even gave it—sent a ripple of unease through me.

"I like knowing people are close," I admitted, choosing my words slowly. "But I don't mind being alone."

She smiled at that, but it didn't quite reach her eyes. "I think I need people. Too much quiet makes me feel like something's waiting."

The way she said it made the hair on my arms rise.

I forced a light laugh. "Waiting for what?"

She shrugged, taking a slow sip of her coffee. "I don't know. Maybe I'll figure it out."

I studied her for a moment. There was something carefully measured about the way she spoke, the way she navigated the conversation as if she were feeling for weak spots.

"Well," I said, standing up, "if you ever need anything, just knock. That's the good thing about a quiet neighborhood—someone's always home."

She nodded, her lips curving just slightly. "Good to know."

As I walked back to my house, I couldn't shake the feeling that I had just stepped into something much bigger than I had realized.

***

That night, as Liam and I sat curled up on the couch, the glow of the TV flickering across the room, he glanced at me out of the corner of his eye. "You've got that look."

I tore my gaze away from the screen. "What look?"

"The I've found something interesting look."

I smirked. "I just think it's strange. Isabella's... different."

Liam sighed, already weary. "Kate—"

"I'm not saying I'm getting involved," I cut in, holding up my hands. "I just don't know what to make of her. She asked me if I ever found this place too quiet."

He frowned. "That's an odd thing to say."

"Right? And it wasn't just that. The way she said it... like she wasn't talking about the neighborhood. More like she was feeling watched."

Liam let out a low chuckle. "Maybe she just needs time to adjust. Not everyone settles in overnight."

I nodded, but something about the conversation with Isabella lingered in my mind, like a half-finished puzzle begging to be solved.

Because the truth was, she wasn't just another new neighbor trying to fit in.

She was something else.

Something I couldn't quite put my finger on.

And I had a feeling I was about to find out.

CHAPTER 2

BUILDING FRIENDSHIP AND SUSPICION

The air was crisp that morning, a soft autumn breeze stirring the golden leaves along the sidewalk. I had just stepped out to grab the newspaper when I spotted Isabella across the street, standing on her porch, staring at something on her phone. She didn't notice me at first—her gaze was locked on the screen, her fingers gripping the edges too tightly. Then, as if sensing she was being watched, she looked up, her blue eyes meeting mine.

A slow, careful smile spread across her lips. "Morning, Kate."

I hesitated before waving. "Morning. Everything okay?"

She blinked, her expression unreadable, before tucking her phone into the pocket of her sweater. "Come have coffee with me."

There was something off in her voice. A tension, a weight.

I glanced back at my house. Liam was still inside, probably enjoying his first cup of the day. I could go back in, pretend I hadn't noticed the way Isabella's fingers trembled when she put her phone away.

Or I could walk across the street.

I sighed and made my decision

***

Her porch smelled of cinnamon and something floral, like an expensive candle burning just inside the house. A sleek silver coffee pot sat between us, along with two delicate white mugs. Isabella poured my cup with a practiced elegance, her hands steadier now.

"I've been meaning to talk to you," she said, stirring her coffee, her voice light but forced.

"About what?" I asked, wrapping my fingers around the warm ceramic.

She glanced toward the street, as if checking for wandering ears, before lowering her voice. "Steven."

I raised an eyebrow. "Your husband?"

She let out a soft, humorless laugh. "Supposedly."

That got my attention. I straightened slightly. "What do you mean?"

Isabella sighed, rubbing her temples. "I know this sounds paranoid, but I think he's seeing someone else."

Her words landed heavily between us.

I studied her carefully. Her expression was tight, her fingers clenching her coffee cup just a little too hard. This wasn't some casual suspicion—she believed it.

"Why do you think that?" I asked carefully.

Instead of answering, she pulled her phone back out and tapped on the screen a few times before handing it to me.

The image was blurry, grainy, like it had been zoomed in too much. A woman, young, with dark hair pulled into a loose ponytail, was stepping out of a car. It wasn't immediately incriminating—just a person caught in motion—but the way Isabella watched me made the moment feel heavier.

"Who is she?" I asked.

"That's what I've been trying to figure out," she murmured. "I saw her once, outside a restaurant Steven was supposed to be at for a business meeting. I didn't think much of it until I saw her again, a few days later, not far from here."

That caught me off guard. "She lives here?"

Isabella nodded, chewing on the inside of her cheek. "I don't know for sure, but I've seen her near the park at the end of the street. It can't be a coincidence." She hesitated, then added, almost as if thinking out loud, "And then there's that blue house…"

I frowned. "What blue house?"

She blinked, as if she hadn't meant to say that. "Nothing, it's just—one time, I saw her near this house on Maple and 7th. It looked empty, but she was standing outside like she was waiting for someone."

I stared at the picture again, but it wasn't much to go on. The woman's face was turned away, her posture casual, unaware that she was being captured as evidence of something she might not even be part of.

"Have you confronted Steven about it?" I asked.

Isabella let out a breathy laugh. "And say what? Hey, I took blurry, stalker-ish photos of a random woman—are you sleeping with her?"

I cracked a small smile despite myself. "Okay, fair. But have you talked to him at all? About your suspicions?"

Her gaze darkened. "Steven is very… good at avoiding things. He has a way of making me feel crazy for even asking questions."

That didn't sit right with me.

She leaned forward slightly, her voice dropping even lower. "What would you do, Kate?"

I hesitated. "If I thought Liam was cheating?"

She nodded.

I exhaled. "I'd get proof. Real proof. And then I'd decide if I wanted to walk away or fight for him."

Her lips parted slightly, as if she hadn't expected that answer. "So you would look?"

"If I needed to," I admitted.

She smiled then. Slow. Almost… pleased.

A shiver crawled up my spine.

"I knew I liked you," she murmured.

I cleared my throat, shifting in my seat. "Look, Isabella, I get why you're suspicious, but don't jump to conclusions just yet. That woman could be anyone."

Her expression flickered with something unreadable before she nodded. "You're right."

But she didn't sound convinced.

***

By the time I got home, my mind was buzzing.

Liam was at the kitchen counter, scrolling through his phone with a half-eaten bagel in front of him. He looked up when I walked in. "How's the new neighbor?"

I hesitated, then pulled out a mug and poured myself some coffee. "She thinks her husband is cheating."

Liam's eyebrows lifted. "That was fast."

"She showed me a picture," I said, blowing on my coffee. "Some woman she saw near Steven's office and then here in our neighborhood."

Liam chewed his bagel thoughtfully. "And?"

"And… I don't know. The whole thing feels weird."

"Weird how?"

I leaned against the counter, staring down at my coffee. "She's so certain, but she doesn't really have proof. And the way she talks about Steven… it's like he's more of a concept than a person."

Liam smirked. "Maybe she watches too many crime shows."

I shot him a look. "I'm serious. Something just doesn't add up."

He sighed, setting his phone down. "Kate, I know that look. Whatever's going on with Isabella and Steven, it's their problem. Not yours."

I opened my mouth to argue, but he raised a hand. "Nope. Don't do that thing where you make this your personal mystery to solve."

I crossed my arms. "I wasn't."

He gave me a flat look.

I huffed. "Fine. But I am keeping my eyes open."

Liam muttered something under his breath before taking another bite of his bagel.

But even as I promised him—and myself—that I wouldn't get involved, a gnawing unease settled in my chest.

Because something about Isabella wasn't right.

And I had a feeling I was about to find out just how deep this went

CHAPTER 3

KATE'S CURIOSITY

I made a promise, both to myself and to Liam, that I wouldn't let my curiosity spiral into something bigger. After all, what harm was there in just letting things unfold?

But then, the more I thought about Isabella's odd comments, the blurry photos of a woman she claimed was Steven's affair, the more that nagging feeling started eating away at me. Something didn't add up, and I couldn't just let it go.

I wasn't going to turn into one of those obsessive, paranoid types. I told myself that. But the itch in my brain kept growing, and when I finally gave in to the temptation of a little casual observation, I tried to convince myself that I was just satisfying my own need for clarity. Nothing major, just a few quiet glances, a little more attention to details.

Nothing serious.

But deep down, I knew I was already in too deep.

***

That evening, Liam and I sat curled up on the couch, a half-empty bowl of popcorn between us. The movie playing was one of those classic, slow-burn romances, the kind that Liam always pretended to hate but secretly enjoyed.

I nudged him playfully. "Admit it, you love this."

He smirked, tossing a piece of popcorn into his mouth. "I tolerate it. For you."

"Oh, so sitting through Titanic three times was just for me?"

He groaned. "You said you wouldn't bring that up again."

I laughed, tucking my feet under me. "I still think it's romantic."

Liam shook his head. "You think people freezing to death is romantic?"

I rolled my eyes. "Not that part. The grand, sweeping love story part."

He wrapped an arm around my shoulders, pulling me closer. "You don't need a shipwreck to have a love story."

I smiled, resting my head against his chest, listening to the steady rhythm of his heartbeat. We stayed like that for a while, wrapped in the warmth of each other, until I broke the comfortable silence with a casual, offhand question.

"Hey, have you ever met Isabella's husband?"

Liam stiffened slightly. "Steven?"

"Yeah."

He was quiet for a moment, then shook his head. "Now that you mention it… no. I don't think I have."

I pulled back slightly to look at him. "Strange, right? I mean, they've been here for weeks, and no one's seen him."

Liam sighed, rubbing a hand over his face. "Kate—"

I held up a hand. "Relax, I'm not starting anything. It just seems… off."

He studied me for a second, then sighed. "You always think something's off."

I smirked. "And am I ever wrong?"

Liam groaned. "I should've let you watch Titanic alone."

I laughed, but as we settled back into our movie, my mind kept circling back to Steven.

***

The next morning, I watched from my front window as Steven's car pulled out of their driveway. A sleek black sedan, polished to perfection.

I checked my watch. 7:15 AM.

The same time he had left yesterday. And the day before that.

So, he was around—at least long enough to leave for work each morning.

I waited another few minutes before stepping outside. Isabella's house was quiet, her curtains drawn.

She had been acting strange lately, more on edge. It made me wonder if she'd been watching Steven leave, too.

I slid into my car and pulled out onto the street, keeping my distance but following the direction Steven had gone. I told myself I wasn't really following him—just… seeing where he went. If he turned toward the business district, then fine. He was at work, and Isabella's suspicions were just that—suspicions.

But if he turned somewhere else…

I tightened my grip on the wheel. Steven drove straight for about ten minutes, then turned left—right toward the office buildings downtown.

I let out a breath I didn't realize I was holding, "Okay, he was at work."

But that still didn't explain Isabella's obsession with this mystery woman.

So, I shifted my focus. I had an address—well, sort of.

The woman in Isabella's picture had supposedly been spotted near the park, which meant she must live somewhere close. Isabella had been vague, but she'd mentioned a blue house with a porch, near the corner of Maple and 7th.

I drove slowly down the quiet residential street, my gaze flicking between house numbers and mailboxes. And then I saw it.

A small, blue house with a wraparound porch, the paint slightly peeling at the edges. It wasn't remarkable, but something about it felt wrong. Maybe it was the overgrown grass or the way the curtains were drawn tightly shut, like they hadn't been touched in months.

I pulled over and sat there for a moment, debating.

Then, before I could overthink it, I got out. I wasn't trespassing exactly—just… checking.

I walked up the short path to the front door and knocked.

No answer.

I knocked again, glancing over my shoulder as if someone might be watching.

Still nothing.

The house felt abandoned. I stepped back and moved toward one of the windows, peeking through a small gap in the curtains. Dust. Empty floors. No furniture.

The place was completely vacant.

I frowned.

Why would Isabella think this woman lived here? Had she ever lived here?

A chill crept up my spine, because something about this wasn't adding up.

As I turned to leave, I noticed the mailbox. It was stuffed with unopened letters, some of them yellowing at the edges. I hesitated before pulling one out just enough to read the name.

No name. Just "Current Resident."

I let the envelope fall back into place, my pulse quickening.

Isabella had been so sure about this woman. So why did it seem like she had never lived here at all?

***

I was still turning it over in my head when I got home. The moment I stepped inside, Bella, our Samoyed mix, perked up from her spot by the door. Her fluffy white fur made her look like a small cloud, but the sharpness in her eyes told a different story. She padded over to me, sniffing my hands like she was searching for clues.

"You went out early," Liam noted from the kitchen, his back to me as he poured himself a cup of coffee.

I forced a smile, trying to keep my mind from spiraling. "Just ran a few errands."

Liam glanced at me briefly. "Hmm."

I could feel Bella's gaze on me as I walked past her, her head tilted slightly, ears pricked. She didn't follow me right away, but I knew she was paying attention. Something about her quiet behavior didn't sit right.

Liam leaned against the counter, taking a sip of his coffee. "What's going on with you two?" he asked, watching Bella stay rooted by the door, her eyes locked on me.

I shrugged, trying to ignore the unease creeping up my spine. "She's just acting strange today."

Liam glanced over at Bella, who was still standing watch. "She doesn't usually act like that."

"No," I agreed, absentmindedly stroking the top of Bella's head as she stood beside me. "It's like she senses something."

Liam shook his head but didn't say anything. After a beat, I decided to take a different approach. "Hey… if someone were lying about something big, would you want to know?"

Liam paused mid-sip, his eyes narrowing just slightly. "That depends. Who's lying?"

I hesitated, not wanting to sound like I was diving into a rabbit hole. "Just... in general."

Liam set his mug down and looked at me, his expression softening. "Kate. What did you do?"

I exhaled slowly, then decided to come clean. "I went to the house Isabella mentioned—the one where she said she saw that woman."

Liam's face shifted immediately, a look of concern crossing his features. "You went there? By yourself?"

"Yeah," I said, trying to sound nonchalant, though I knew that was far from how I felt. "It was empty. No one's been living there for months."

Liam's frown deepened, and he leaned forward, rubbing his face. "Why would she say she saw someone there if the house is abandoned?"

"I don't know," I muttered. "But I need to figure out why she would lie about something like that. It just doesn't add up."

Bella, who had been pacing around my legs, suddenly stopped and gave a low growl. I froze.

Liam looked at her, his voice quiet. "What's she doing?"

I held my breath, watching Bella as she lowered her body to the ground, her eyes fixed on the door like she was waiting for something to appear. Her tail flicked back and forth just once, then stopped.

"She's acting… off," I said, slowly kneeling down to pet her, but Bella took a step back, almost like she was warning me. She looked up at me, her gaze sharp, almost anxious.

Liam noticed the change in the air too. "She's never like this. What do you think it means?"

I stood up, still unsettled by Bella's sudden wariness. "I don't know, but she doesn't trust Isabella. It's like she knows something we don't."

Liam glanced between me and the dog. "Kate, I get that you're trying to make sense of all this, but—"

"Liam, it doesn't make sense," I interrupted, my voice a little sharper than I intended. "I saw the house, and now I'm thinking Isabella's hiding something. What if she's not telling the truth?"

Liam's expression softened, but he didn't seem convinced. "Maybe she's just confused, Kate. Maybe she saw the woman near the house and assumed—"

"I saw the house, Liam," I snapped. "It's been vacant for months."

Bella let out a soft whimper, curling up at my feet and looking up at me with those deep, soulful eyes. Her behavior was making me even more certain that I wasn't just chasing a hunch. Something wasn't right, and Bella felt it too.

Liam sighed, stepping back and running a hand through his hair. "Okay, I get it. You're worried. But there's not much more we can do."

I tried to push my doubts aside, and go about my normal routine, pretend I wasn't questioning every single thing Isabella had told me.

But the thing about doubt? Once it creeps in, it's impossible to ignore.

***

The next time I saw Isabella, she was standing in her front yard, carefully trimming the edges of a rose bush. She looked up as I approached, flashing that effortless, magazine-perfect smile.

"Hey," I greeted, folding my arms as I leaned against the fence.

"Hi, Kate." She wiped a gloved hand across her forehead, though I noticed there wasn't a single speck of dirt on her. "You're up early."

"Could say the same about you," I replied lightly.

She let out a soft laugh, but there was something distant about it. "Couldn't sleep."

I hesitated before asking, "Steven home?"

Her smile faltered—just for a fraction of a second, but I caught it.

"No, he had to leave on a last-minute trip," she said smoothly, turning her attention back to the roses.

Another trip? I glanced at their driveway. Empty.

"Must be exhausting," I commented, watching her carefully. "Him always being away."

She nodded but didn't elaborate, and that was the first red flag.

Isabella loved to talk—about the town, the people, her thoughts on the latest bestseller. But when it came to Steven? Nothing. No details about their life together, no stories about how they met or their wedding.

Just vague, clipped answers.

I pushed a little further. "Where'd he go this time?"

She hesitated, just for a second too long. 'San Francisco'

There was something rehearsed about the way she said it, like she had practiced the answer beforehand.

I let the silence stretch between us, waiting to see if she'd fill it, but she didn't. Instead, she adjusted her gardening gloves, her expression unreadable.

The Isabella I had first met had been charming, warm, inviting.

But this Isabella? She felt like a locked door I wasn't supposed to open.

***

That night, as Liam and I sat at the kitchen table, I finally voiced what had been rattling around in my head.

"Did you know they're raising property taxes again?" I said, stabbing at my salad with unnecessary force.

Liam glanced up, already looking wary. "I did. You gonna start a neighborhood revolt?"

"Maybe," I muttered. "It's ridiculous. They're claiming it's for 'community improvements,' but have you seen the potholes on Maple Street? I nearly lost a tire the other day."

Liam smirked. "You do drive like you're fleeing a crime scene."

I shot him a look. "Excuse me for respecting efficiency."

He chuckled, reaching for his glass of water. "I don't know, Kate. Maybe the town is just slow with repairs. Bureaucracy and all that."

I rolled my eyes. "That's the kind of attitude that lets them get away with it. We should demand answers."

Liam held up a hand. "By all means. Draft your angry letter. Start your revolution."

I pointed my fork at him. "Don't tempt me."

He grinned, taking a bite of his food. "Anything else bothering you, or is local government your only target tonight?"

I hesitated.

And then, as if the thought had been waiting just beneath the surface, I blurted out, "Something's off with Isabella."

Liam groaned. "And here we go."

"Just listen," I pressed. "She barely talks about Steven. Like, at all. And when I asked where he was, she hesitated. Like she had to think about it first."

Liam set his fork down and pinched the bridge of his nose. "Maybe because you caught her off guard? Maybe she's just tired of explaining why her husband is always gone?"

"Or maybe," I countered, leaning forward, "she's lying."

Liam let out a slow breath. "Kate, I love you. But you have a habit of seeing mysteries where there aren't any."

I opened my mouth to argue, but he raised a hand to stop me.

"I'm not saying you're wrong," he added carefully. "I'm just saying… maybe take a step back before you go full-on detective mode, okay?"

I huffed. "I'm not in detective mode."

Liam gave me a look.

I sighed. "Fine. I'll drop it."

(Again, I absolutely did not drop it.)

***

A couple days went by, and I saw Isabella, she was in her backyard, sitting on the patio with a glass of wine. She looked different—tired, distracted.

I debated whether to approach her, but my curiosity won.

"Rough day?" I asked, sliding into the chair across from her.

She startled slightly before recovering, offering me a small smile. "You could say that."

She took a slow sip of wine, her fingers drumming lightly against the glass.

Then, out of nowhere, she asked, "Do you ever feel like people only show you what they want you to see?"

The question threw me. "Yeah, I guess," I said carefully. "Why?"

She let out a small, humorless laugh. "Just something I've been thinking about."

I watched her, the way she stared at nothing in particular, lost in thought.

"Is this about Steven?" I asked gently.

She tensed, just for a second, before shaking her head. "No. It's just… life, I suppose."

I knew she was lying, and now I had more questions than ever.

***

That night, I couldn't shake the feeling that I was missing something big. So, I did what I probably shouldn't have done—I checked Steven's car.

It was late, the neighborhood quiet as I slipped across the yard, sticking to the shadows. Isabella's house was dark, no lights on. The sedan sat in the driveway, just like always. I reached out, fingers brushing the handle. Locked. Of course.

But as I stepped back, something caught my eye—something wedged between the windshield wipers. A parking ticket.

I leaned in, squinting at the date. Issued this morning.

Isabella had said Steven was in San Francisco. So why was his car parked in town this morning?

CHAPTER 4

MYSTERY MAN OR WOMAN?

Isabella had always been friendly, but something about her felt guarded—like she was keeping people at arm's length. That's why, when she called and asked if I could come over to help her pick a dress for her birthday, I was surprised.

Still, I agreed. Not just because I was curious, but because the nagging feeling in my gut wouldn't go away. The parking ticket. The abandoned house. The inconsistencies in her stories. It all sat heavy in the back of my mind, whispering that something wasn't right.

So, I went.

Isabella greeted me at the door with a bright smile, her hair swept into a loose bun. "Thank you for coming," she said, ushering me inside. "I need a second opinion. I feel like everything I own is either too formal or too casual."

"No problem," I said, stepping in and glancing around. The house was as pristine as ever, not a single thing out of place.

She sighed dramatically, leading me toward the living room. "Steven isn't around, of course. Work has him tied up, as usual." She rolled her eyes but smiled as she continued, "So, he planned a dinner for me in advance—said he knew that if he didn't, I'd probably spend the day rotting in bed."

I let out a small laugh. "That does sound like you."

"Right?" she said, plopping onto the couch beside me. "He promised to be available virtually during dinner tonight, though. Apparently, tomorrow—on my actual birthday—he's stuck in back-to-back meetings."

I tilted my head. "That's sweet, though. At least he's making an effort."

She waved a hand. "Yeah, yeah. It's something, I guess. But let's be real, it's not the same as having him here." She sighed, then brightened. "Anyway, that's why I need your help. If I'm going to be wined and dined—virtually or not—I need to look stunning."

I smiled, nodding toward the hallway. "Alright, let's see what you've got

Her house smelled like lavender and vanilla—warm, inviting, yet oddly impersonal. I followed her into the bedroom, where a few dresses were laid out across the bed. A deep red one, a sleek black one, and a soft blue one that looked like it belonged in a fairy tale.

"What do you think?" Isabella asked, holding up the blue one against herself.

I tilted my head. "Depends. Are we going for elegant or 'I just threw this on and happened to look amazing'?"

She laughed. "Somewhere in between."

Before I could answer, she let out a dramatic sigh. "Ugh, I need to fix my eyeliner. Be right back." She grabbed a small makeup pouch from the dresser and disappeared into the bathroom, the door clicking shut behind her.

I turned back to the dresses, running my fingers over the fabric absentmindedly.

That's when I saw it.

A stack of papers sat on the nightstand—receipts, slightly crumpled, as if they had been shoved there in a hurry. I knew I shouldn't, but my curiosity got the best of me. I picked up the top one, scanning the date.

Three months ago.

A second one. Four months ago.

A third. Six months.

My stomach twisted.

Isabella had told me they'd only moved in a few weeks ago. But these weren't just old receipts—they were recent purchases from local stores. She had been here for months.

I reached for the drawer beneath the nightstand, my heart hammering.

It wasn't fully closed, just slightly ajar. Like someone had been in a hurry and didn't push it all the way in.

Carefully, I pulled it open.

Inside, a stack of photographs. I grabbed one from the middle, my breath catching as I took it in.

It was Isabella's house—her driveway, to be exact. But the car parked there wasn't Steven's like I had assumed. It was the same one I'd been watching all along, the one I thought belonged to her elusive husband.

And in the reflection of the side mirror, a blurry figure stood near the driver's side. Dressed in dark clothes, posture stiff. At first glance, it looked like a man.

But the longer I stared, the details sharpened. The familiar tilt of the head, the sleeves hanging just a little too long - and I realized it wasn't Steven; it was Isabella.

And the date stamped in the corner? Five months ago.

I barely had time to process it before I heard the bathroom door creak open.

Shit.

I shoved the photo back, slammed the drawer shut, and spun toward the bed, grabbing the nearest pair of heels and holding them up like I'd been studying them the whole time.

"Maybe these?" I said, forcing my voice to stay even.

Isabella walked back into the room, wiping the corner of her eye where her eyeliner must have smudged. She glanced at the shoes in my hand and smiled.

"You have good taste," she said, taking them from me.

I let out a quiet breath of relief, nodding like everything was perfectly normal. But my mind was racing.

She had lied about when she moved in, about Steven's car, and now I had proof—but why?

I left Isabella's house with my thoughts tangled in knots.

The receipts. The photos. The car.

Isabella had been living there for months—long before she claimed she moved in. And if she was lying about that, what else was she lying about?

I clenched my fists as I walked up the driveway, unease creeping up my spine. Bella, my fluffy white Samoyed, barked excitedly from the yard, her tail wagging like a manic metronome. But as I stepped closer, a strange tension settled over me - the gate was closed.

Bella was always inside when I left—never locked in the yard.

I walked over quickly, my pulse picking up. "Hey, girl," I murmured, reaching for the latch. It was shut tight. Not just closed— latched from the outside. Someone had put her there.

My eyes flicked toward Isabella's house.

And that's when I saw her.

Standing at her bedroom window, barely visible through the sheer curtains. Watching.

The moment our eyes met, she turned away, like she hadn't been staring at all.

I swallowed hard, trying to shake the creeping unease curling in my stomach. Was I imagining things? Overreacting?

I unlatched the gate, and Bella trotted out, rubbing against my legs like she hadn't just been trapped outside.

Liam's car wasn't in the driveway yet, so I went inside and paced the kitchen, my mind buzzing.

Isabella was lying.

She had been watching.

And somehow, my dog had ended up locked in the yard.

I grabbed a glass of water, but my hands were still shaking.

Fifteen minutes later, Liam walked through the front door, tossing his keys onto the counter. "Hey."

I turned, struggling to keep my voice casual. "Hey."

His gaze flicked to Bella, who had curled up by the back door. "Why was she outside?"

I hesitated. "I don't know. The gate was latched when I got home."

Liam frowned, immediately alert. "You think someone put her there?"

I opened my mouth, then closed it again. The words felt ridiculous. What was I going to say? I think our neighbor locked our dog outside and then stared at me through the window like a psychopath?

Instead, I sighed. "Maybe I forgot to bring her in this morning."

Liam studied me, unconvinced, but he let it go. "You okay? You look… I don't know. Edgy."

I hesitated again, then shook my head. "It's probably nothing."

He gave me a look. "Kate."

I exhaled. "Okay. It's Isabella."

Liam groaned before I even finished. "Kate, no."

"She lied," I said quickly. "About when they moved in. I found receipts from months ago. And photos of her house with her car in the driveway from before they supposedly got here."

Liam pinched the bridge of his nose. "You went through her stuff?"

"Not on purpose," I said defensively. "She left it out."

"That's not the point," he said, shaking his head. "You're getting involved again."

I scowled. "This is different."

"Is it?" His voice was pointed now. "Because last time, you swore that was different, too. And remind me how that ended?"

A sharp pang of guilt shot through me.

I didn't like to talk about it.

About the last time my curiosity got the best of me.

Liam crossed his arms. "I'm just saying, maybe—maybe—you don't go digging around in things that don't concern you."

I folded my arms right back. "And what if they do concern me?"

Liam let out a frustrated breath. "Kate—"

But I was already shaking my head.

"I'm not saying I'm going to do anything crazy," I lied. "I just think something's off, and I don't like not knowing why."

Liam sighed, rubbing a hand over his face. "Just… be careful. Please."

I nodded, but I wasn't letting this go. Everything about this felt off, and I was going to uncover the truth.

CHAPTER 5

THE CONFRONTATION

I wasn't proud of what I was about to do.

Standing on Isabella's porch, I hesitated, my pulse drumming in my ears. The house was quiet, the curtains drawn, just like always. From the outside, nothing seemed out of place. But I knew better now.

Isabella had been lying to me.

For months, she had been living here in secret, pretending to move in only when she was ready to be seen. And then there was Steven— her supposedly devoted husband, who was never around, never mentioned except in passing. Yet, for all her talk, I had never once seen a picture of them together.

My fingers tightened around the doorknob. I didn't expect it to turn, but when it did, a rush of cold dread ran through me. Unlocked.

She either didn't think anyone would dare snoop, or she had left in a hurry. Either way, this was my chance.

I stepped inside, closing the door softly behind me.

***

The house was eerily still, save for the faint hum of the refrigerator. A subtle lavender scent lingered in the air, the kind that came from one of those overpriced candles Isabella liked to keep burning. Everything was neat—too neat. No clutter, no stray dishes in the sink, no shoes by the door. It felt staged, like a showroom rather than a home.

I moved cautiously through the living room, scanning the walls. That was the first thing that struck me—there were no photographs. None of Steven, none of Isabella. Just generic art prints, the kind you'd buy to fill space.

A strange feeling twisted in my gut.

I drifted toward the bookshelf, running my fingers along the spines. Everything was arranged meticulously, alphabetized even. That wasn't strange in itself—but then I noticed the gaps. Certain books looked like they had been pulled and replaced hastily, their edges misaligned.

My hands trembled slightly as I slid one out.

Tucked between the pages was a folded piece of paper.

Unfolding it carefully, I found a printout of a rental agreement— not for this house, but for a different address. My breath caught as I read the name at the top.

Isabella Monroe.

But that wasn't right. Her last name was supposed to be Davis.

I reached for another book. Another document. Another name.

Isabella Harrington.

Isabella Greene.

Each one different, each tied to a different address, a different life.

I swallowed hard, my mind spinning.

Who the hell was she?

*****

I moved deeper into the house, my footsteps careful against the hardwood. The bedroom door was slightly ajar. Taking a steadying breath, I slipped inside.

More of the same. Too clean, too precise. The bed was made perfectly, the pillows fluffed like a hotel. No sign of Steven's things— no men's shoes, no clothes, not even an extra toothbrush in the bathroom.

I pulled open the closet, sifting through the hanging clothes.

Then I saw them—the photographs.

Not framed or displayed, but tucked in a shoebox on the top shelf. I reached up, pulling it down with shaky hands.

Flipping through them, my stomach turned.

In each one, Isabella looked different.

Her hair, her clothes, even her posture changed from picture to picture. In some, she had dark curls framing her face, a confident smirk. In others, she was blonde, dressed in soft pastels, her expression demure.

It was like looking at different people.

But the eyes… the eyes were always the same.

I clenched my jaw, trying to make sense of it.

Was she running from someone? Hiding? Or was it something worse?

A stack of utility bills sat on the nightstand. I flipped through them, my pulse spiking as I caught the dates.

Five months ago. Six.

I inhaled sharply.

She had been here all along.

***

A floorboard creaked.

I froze.

The front door clicked shut, the sound slicing through the silence like a knife. My breath hitched as I whipped my head toward the bedroom door. She wasn't supposed to be home yet.

Panic clawed at my throat as I scrambled to put everything back the way I found it. I shoved the shoebox onto the shelf, smoothed the nightstand drawer shut with barely a whisper of sound, and turned in search of an escape. The window was too high, the closet too obvious, and before I could decide whether I could make it out of the bedroom unseen, footsteps echoed down the hall.

They slowed outside the door. A pause. A breath.

Then, the handle turned.

I had no choice. I darted into the bathroom, pressing myself against the wall just as Isabella stepped inside the bedroom.

Silence.

I squeezed my eyes shut, willing my breathing to steady. Then I heard it—the closet door sliding open. A rustling, followed by a sudden, sharp thud. My heart pounded. She knew something was off. She was checking. I could practically feel her suspicion thickening the air.

I needed a cover. Fast.

My gaze landed on the vanity, where a glass bottle of perfume sat untouched. I reached for it, twisting the cap with a deliberate click before stepping into the doorway like I had been there the whole time.

Isabella whirled toward me, her dark eyes flashing, her posture unnervingly still. For a moment, she didn't speak. She just stared at me, taking in every detail—my hand on the perfume, the slight tension in my shoulders, the faint flush of my skin. I forced a casual smile.

"Hey," I said, holding up the bottle like it was the most normal thing in the world. "I, uh… ran out of perfume at home. Thought I'd borrow some."

Her expression didn't change. She barely even blinked.

"That's funny," she murmured. "Because I just found my closet door open."

My stomach lurched.

She took a slow step forward, tilting her head slightly. "And the nightstand drawer wasn't how I left it."

I gripped the perfume bottle tighter, my mind racing for an excuse. "I must've bumped into something. You know me—clumsy."

Her lips curled into a slow smile, but there was no warmth in it. "Clumsy," she echoed, as if testing the word on her tongue.

Before I could react, she reached past me and pressed the bathroom door shut with a quiet click. The sound sent a chill down my spine. I was trapped. The walls of the bedroom suddenly felt too close, the air too thin.

"You were snooping." It wasn't a question.

I opened my mouth, but nothing came out. Because she was right.

She let out a soft, almost amused sigh and shook her head. "Kate, Kate, Kate…" Her voice was gentle, chiding. "You just couldn't leave it alone, could you?"

I forced myself to stand my ground, though every instinct screamed at me to run. "I just… I noticed some things didn't add up," I said carefully. "The move-in date. Steven's car. And then I realized—there's nothing of his here. No pictures, no clothes. It's like he doesn't exist."

Her smile didn't waver, but something flickered behind her eyes.

"I told you, Steven travels a lot."

"Then why lie about when you moved in?" I pressed.

For the first time, something flickered across her face—gone in an instant, but I saw it. A crack in the carefully constructed mask. But instead of panic, her expression smoothed into something almost… disappointed.

"Well," she murmured, almost to herself. "That's inconvenient."

Inconvenient.

Not shocking. Not upsetting. Just a problem to be handled.

A chill settled deep in my bones.

"I think you should leave," she said, her voice soft but firm.

I didn't move.

Her fingers twitched at her sides, subtle but telling. She was waiting to see if I'd hesitate, if I'd defy her.

I swallowed hard and took a step toward the door. She mirrored me, closing the distance just slightly, just enough to make my skin prickle.

The moment I reached the hallway, she spoke again. "You should be careful, Kate."

Something in her tone made my breath catch. I turned my head just enough to see the smile stretching across her lips, too slow, too knowing.

"People might start thinking you're obsessed with me."

A sick feeling coiled in my stomach.

The shift in her tone made my blood run cold.

She wasn't angry. She wasn't even surprised.

She was amused.

Like she had been waiting for this.

Waiting for me to figure it out.

"I think you should go now, Kate," she said, still smiling.

My throat felt dry.

"Isabella—"

Her head tilted slightly.

"You should go."

The room suddenly felt smaller, the air too thick. I forced myself to nod, to act normal, even as every instinct screamed at me to run.

I turned for the door, my hand gripping the knob.

But before I stepped out, I hesitated.

"I just have one more question," I said, my voice quiet.

She waited.

"The different names. The different looks. Who are you really?"

A long pause. Then, with a ghost of a smirk, she said,

"I guess you'll have to figure that out, too."

***

I walked out of that house with my heart in my throat.

The night air hit me like a slap, but it wasn't enough to shake the chill that had settled in my bones.

I had gone looking for answers, and I had found them.

But now, I had even more questions.

And worse—

I had the sinking feeling Isabella knew exactly what I'd do next.

And she was waiting for it.

***

I barely slept that night.

Every time I closed my eyes, I saw Isabella's face—her too-calm smile, the sharp glint in her eyes when she told me to leave. She knew. She knew I had figured her out, and worse, she wasn't afraid.

No, she was enjoying this.

By morning, my stomach was in knots. I was halfway through my second cup of coffee when my phone buzzed.

Liam: Hey, everything okay? "I ran into Isabella when leaving for work". She seemed… upset.

A cold knot formed in my chest. I stared at the message, my fingers tightening around the mug.

Isabella had wasted no time.

I tapped out a quick response—What did she say?—but before I could hit send, there was a sharp knock at my door.

I already knew who it was.

Taking a slow breath, I walked to the door and opened it.

Isabella stood there, arms crossed, expression perfectly composed. But there was something different now—something calculated.

"We need to talk," she said.

I stepped aside, letting her in. She moved past me like she owned the place, her gaze sweeping the room.

""I saw Liam this morning," she said, turning back to face me. "I told him I was worried about you."

I stiffened. "Worried?"

She tilted her head, feigning sympathy. "You've been acting… strange. Obsessive, even. Digging into things that aren't your business."

A sharp pang of anger flared in my chest. "I was looking for the truth."

She sighed, shaking her head. "The truth?" A small, mocking smile played on her lips. "Kate, I don't know what's going on with you, but it's starting to scare me. First, you break into my house, then you start spinning these insane theories? About me? About Steven?"

My hands curled into fists. "I didn't break in. The door was unlocked."

She waved a hand dismissively. "Doesn't matter. The fact is, you were snooping. And now, you're trying to turn everyone against me."

I sucked in a sharp breath. "That's not what I—"

She cut me off. "Liam is worried about you. I told him I was, too. And the neighbors?" She let out a light laugh. "Well, you know how people talk."

My stomach dropped.

I knew exactly what she was doing.

She was isolating me. Twisting the story before I had a chance to tell it myself.

"Don't do this," I said quietly.

Her eyes darkened, the fake concern slipping away. "You brought this on yourself."

***

It didn't take long for the shift to happen.

By the end of the week, I could feel the stares. The whispers. The polite but distant smiles from neighbors who had once stopped to chat.

Liam had been the hardest.

I had tried to explain, tried to make him see what Isabella was doing, but the damage was already done.

"She seemed genuinely scared, Kate," he had said, brow furrowed. "And honestly? I don't know what to think. You admit you went through her stuff. That's not normal."

I had opened my mouth to argue, to tell him everything, but then I saw it—that flicker of doubt in his eyes.

Isabella had gotten to him.

And now, no matter what I said, I was the one who looked unhinged.

***

A few days later, I was at the grocery store when it happened again.

I had just grabbed a carton of milk when I heard the voice behind me—loud enough for everyone nearby to hear.

"I don't know what I did to make you hate me, Kate, but this has to stop."

I turned slowly, my blood running cold.

Isabella stood there, arms wrapped around herself, eyes wide and wounded. A perfect performance.

People were already looking.

"You're following me," she said, voice trembling just enough. "You're harassing me. I just want to live my life, but you won't let me."

A middle-aged woman in the aisle glanced between us, frowning. A store employee shifted uncomfortably nearby.

I took a slow breath, keeping my voice level. "I came here for groceries, Isabella. Just like you."

She let out a humorless laugh, shaking her head. "Right. Just like how you 'accidentally' ended up in my house?"

Murmurs rippled through the aisle.

My heart pounded. She was baiting me—trying to make me snap, to give everyone watching proof that I was the problem.

I forced myself to stay calm. "I think you should go."

Her expression flickered. Just for a second.

She had wanted a reaction. A fight. And I hadn't given her one.

With a sharp inhale, she turned on her heel and walked away, leaving behind a trail of curious stares.

I exhaled slowly, gripping the shopping cart so tightly my knuckles ached.

She was winning.

And I had no idea how to stop her.

That night, I sat in my living room, staring at my phone.

I had taken pictures of the documents I found in her house. Proof of her lies. But showing them to people now? It wouldn't work. Not after everything she had done to discredit me.

I needed something bigger.

Something undeniable.

My mind raced through everything I knew about her, about Steven. The receipts. The fake names. The missing husband.

And then it hit me.

The one thing I had never thought to check.

The house.

Not the inside, not the lies Isabella had woven around it—but the actual house itself.

The records. The ownership. The history.

If Isabella had been hiding for months before she "moved in," there had to be a paper trail. A lease, a deed—something.

Grabbing my laptop, I pulled up the county property records. My fingers flew over the keyboard, heart pounding as I typed in the address.

The page loaded, and I froze.

My breath caught in my throat.

Primary Resident: Isabella Harrington.

Not Isabella Davis.

Not even Isabella Monroe.

Harrington.

The same name I had found on one of the old rental agreements.

A name she had abandoned.

But why?

And then I saw it.

Buried deep in the records, in a section most people wouldn't think to check.

Prior Owner: Lillian Harrington.

The last name was the same.

I clicked on it, scanning for details.

My stomach dropped.

Lillian Harrington—deceased.

A former owner of the house.

And she had died inside it.

My pulse thundered in my ears.

Isabella hadn't just moved in early.

She had always been here.

***

I barely had time to process it before my phone buzzed.

A new message.

From an unknown number.

Stop.

Just one word.

But it was enough to send ice through my veins.

I glanced toward the window, my breath shallow. The blinds were drawn, but suddenly, I felt exposed.

Like someone was watching.

I had been looking for proof.

And now, someone knew.

I didn't sleep that night.

Because for the first time since this all started—

I was terrified of what I might find next.

CHAPTER 6

FIGHT FOR SURVIVAL

The text came late in the evening, just as I was pouring myself a glass of wine, my hands still shaky from everything I had uncovered.

Isabella: We need to talk. Come alone.

I stared at the screen, my gut twisting. Every alarm bell in my head told me to ignore it, to block her number, to walk away from whatever trap she was setting. But I knew that wasn't an option. Not after what I had found in her house. Not after the way she had looked at me when she caught me snooping.

She wasn't done with me. And the truth was, I wasn't done with her either.

A second message followed, this time with a location pinned just outside of town.

The cliffs.

My breath hitched. It was an isolated stretch of rocky terrain just past the old highway, a place where the ground crumbled dangerously close to the edge, where the drop into the dark water below was nothing short of deadly.

I clenched my jaw.

She wanted control. She wanted me on her terms, her turf. And I was walking straight into it.

But I wasn't going in blind.

I grabbed my phone and scrolled to Liam's number, pressing the call button with shaky fingers. The line rang once, then cut to voicemail. I frowned and tried again. Nothing. His phone was off.

"Come on, Liam, pick up," I muttered, my pulse quickening.

I hesitated for only a second before opening our messages and typing quickly.

Kate: Going to meet Isabella at the cliffs. If I don't text you back soon, something's wrong.

I hovered over the send button, then added another line.

Kate: And if anything happens to me, I was right about her.

I exhaled slowly, pressing send. A confirmation popped up—Message delivered.

At least if things went south, someone would know where I was.

Tossing my phone into my bag, I grabbed my car keys and headed out into the night, my heart hammering against my ribs.

***

The drive was suffocatingly silent. My fingers clenched the wheel, knuckles white, as I followed the winding road away from the town's warm glow, deeper into the suffocating dark. The air grew colder, the trees thinning into open space. Wind howled across the cliffside, a sharp, eerie whistle through the rocks.

When I pulled up, her car was already there. A sleek black sedan, headlights off, parked just before the edge.

Isabella stood a few feet away, back to me, the hem of her coat whipping in the wind. There was something unnervingly still about her, like she was waiting—like she had been waiting for a long time.

I stepped out, keeping my distance.

"You really went all out for the dramatic setting," I said, forcing my voice to stay level despite the fear tightening in my chest.

Slowly, she turned. The moonlight carved sharp angles into her face, casting shadows that made her look almost… unreal. And then she smiled. That same slow, knowing smile that made my stomach twist.

"I knew you'd come," she murmured.

Her voice was softer than I expected, almost… pleased. Like she had been hoping for this moment.

I folded my arms, studying her. Something was different tonight— the way she stood, the ease in her posture. She wasn't defensive. She wasn't nervous. She looked—excited.

"You lied," I said, cutting straight to it. "About everything."

Her smile didn't falter. "I told you what you needed to hear."

I scoffed, stepping closer. "You faked moving in. You used different names. You don't even have a husband, do you?"

She tilted her head, considering me. Then, slowly, she shook it. "No," she admitted. "Steven doesn't exist. Never did."

I exhaled sharply, even though I had expected it. Hearing her say it out loud sent a chill down my spine.

"Then who the hell are you?"

Her smile widened, but this time, there was no warmth behind it. "I could ask you the same thing, Kate."

My stomach twisted. "What do you want from me?"

Her expression darkened, amusement slipping away. "I want you to stop," she said simply. "To drop this little obsession before it gets you hurt."

I swallowed. "Is that a threat?"

Her gaze held mine, unblinking. "It's a promise."

A sharp gust of wind whipped past us, the sound of the waves crashing below filling the silence.

I clenched my fists, taking another step. "You don't get to decide how this ends. I know what you've done."

Her jaw tensed. "No," she said softly. "You think you know. But there's so much you don't see, Kate. So much you don't understand."

"Then why don't you explain it to me?" I shot back.

For the first time, her mask cracked. A flicker of something unhinged, something raw, flashed in her eyes. And then she laughed. A quiet, breathy sound that sent ice down my spine.

"You still think you're in control, don't you?" she murmured, stepping closer. "You think you've figured it all out."

I forced myself to hold my ground. "I know you're not who you say you are. I know you've been here longer than you claimed. I know you're dangerous."

Her lips parted slightly, her breath hitching like I had said something she didn't expect. And then, just as quickly, she smiled again.

"You're right about one thing," she said, voice dropping to a whisper. "I am dangerous."

She took another step, and my instincts screamed at me to move, to run, but I didn't.

"You think I just appeared in this town by accident?" she continued, her voice like silk, wrapping around me. "That I chose this house, this life, at random?"

A shiver crawled up my spine. "What are you talking about?"

Her smile stretched wider. "I knew you were here, Kate. I knew everything about you before we even met."

My blood turned to ice.

"I watched you," she went on, voice eerily calm. "Before I ever knocked on your door. Before I ever moved into that house. Before you ever suspected me."

"You're lying," I whispered, but the words barely made it past my lips.

She tilted her head, studying me like I was something fascinating. "Am I?"

I shook my head, refusing to let her get in my head. "Why?" I demanded. "Why me?"

Her eyes darkened. "Because you were easy," she said. "Because you wanted to believe me. Because you wanted a friend."

I swallowed hard, nausea rising.

"But then," she sighed, almost disappointed, "you got too nosy."

She took another step, and suddenly, I was hyper-aware of how close to the edge we were. How alone.

"You were supposed to trust me," she said, her voice turning sharp. "We were supposed to be the same."

"I will never be like you," I hissed.

She exhaled through her nose, shaking her head like I had let her down.

"That's a shame," she murmured.

Then she lunged.

The impact sent me stumbling back, my feet skidding against the loose gravel. I barely caught myself before I hit the ground, Isabella's hands already reaching for me again.

She was stronger than she looked, her fingers digging into my arms as she shoved me toward the edge.

My back hit the guardrail.

Panic surged through me as I grabbed at her wrists, trying to push her off. "Isabella, stop!" I gasped.

She didn't.

Her expression twisted, eyes wild. "You should've left it alone, Kate!" she hissed.

I struggled against her grip, kicking out, twisting, anything to break free. My heel caught the side of her knee, and she let out a sharp curse, stumbling back just enough for me to shove her off.

She staggered, catching herself, but the loose gravel beneath her feet shifted dangerously.

I watched it happen in slow motion—the moment she realized the ground wasn't steady, the way her arms flailed as she tried to regain balance. Her gaze met mine, and for the briefest second, there was something almost pleading in her expression.

Then, the earth gave way beneath her.

Her body tipped backward.

I lunged, reaching for her, but it was too late.

She fell.

The scream that tore from her throat was swallowed by the wind as she plunged over the edge.

I stumbled forward, breathless, gripping the guardrail as I peered down into the darkness. The waves churned violently below, the jagged rocks barely visible in the moonlight.

There was no sign of her.

No sound. No movement. She was gone.

***

My breath came in shallow gasps as I staggered back from the railing, my hands trembling violently. The sound of the waves crashing against the jagged rocks below roared in my ears, but I barely registered it. My mind was stuck, spinning in an endless loop of what had just happened.

Isabella was gone.

I forced myself to move, fumbling for my phone with shaking fingers. Just as I unlocked the screen, it buzzed in my hand. Liam.

For a split second, I couldn't breathe.

I swallowed hard and answered.

"Kate?" His voice was sharp, wide awake despite the late hour. "What the hell is going on? You sent me your location and then— nothing. Are you okay?"

I opened my mouth, but no words came out at first. My throat felt tight, like I'd been strangled, my pulse hammering too fast.

"Liam," I finally croaked. "I— I need you to come. Now." I sucked in a ragged breath. "It's Isabella. She—she fell. Off the cliff."

Silence.

Then, his voice dropped, steady but urgent. "Are you fine?"

I blinked, like I was only now realizing I was still standing, still breathing. My skin burned where her nails had dug in, and my legs felt weak, but I was here.

"I'm fine," I whispered.

"I'm on my way," he said immediately. "Stay where you are. Do not move."

The call ended, and I let out a shuddering breath, my entire body trembling. I wrapped my arms around myself, trying to still the shaking, but the cold night air wasn't the problem.

Minutes stretched into what felt like hours. Every gust of wind made me flinch, every shadow had my heart jumping to my throat. My ears strained, half-expecting to hear footsteps, to see Isabella climbing back up, her unhinged grin twisting in the darkness.

But she didn't.

Instead, headlights cut through the night. Liam's car skidded to a stop a few feet away, and before I could even move, he was out, rushing toward me.

"Kate!" His hands gripped my arms, his gaze sweeping over me. "Are you hurt?"

I shook my head, though my entire body felt battered. "I'm fine. But she's—she's gone." I turned, pointing toward the cliff's edge. "She—she tried to kill me, Liam. We fought. I—" My voice broke. "She lost her footing. I tried to grab her, but she—"

His arms tightened around me, grounding me. "Hey, hey, breathe. Just breathe."

I sucked in a shaky breath, my fingers digging into his jacket as if letting go would send me spiraling.

Liam glanced toward the edge, his jaw tightening. Then, after a beat, he pulled out his own phone.

"I'm calling the police," he said, his voice steady, firm. "We're doing this the right way."

A lump formed in my throat, but I nodded.

There was no running from this.

The next few minutes passed in a blur—Liam speaking in clipped tones to dispatch, me barely processing his words. My mind kept replaying the fall, the way Isabella's eyes widened in shock, the desperate grasp of her fingers just before the ground gave way.

A part of me expected her body to be down there, lifeless against the rocks.

Another part of me wasn't so sure.

Liam stayed by my side, his presence the only thing keeping me from completely unraveling.

When the distant wail of sirens finally filled the air, I closed my eyes and let out a breath.

It was over.

Or at least, that's what I told myself.

I didn't stop until I saw the first glimmers of town, the neon signs glowing in the distance, civilization pulling me back from whatever nightmare I had just escaped.

CHAPTER 7

SECRETS DISCOVERED

I sat on the edge of our couch, my hands wrapped around a mug of tea I had no intention of drinking. The warmth barely reached my fingers. Across from me, Liam paced the living room, his arms crossed, his jaw clenched so tightly I could hear the grind of his teeth.

The police had come and gone, their voices still echoing in my head. Questions. So many questions. My story had been simple—I told them the truth, or at least, the version that made sense: Isabella and I met at the cliffs, things escalated, she attacked me, and in the struggle… she fell.

They didn't say much after that. Just exchanged unreadable glances before one of them assured me that they'd be conducting a full investigation.

That was hours ago. And now, I was left here, sitting in the dim glow of our house, my body still thrumming with leftover adrenaline.

Liam suddenly stopped pacing and turned to me. "You need to sleep."

I huffed out something that wasn't quite a laugh. "Yeah, because that's gonna happen."

His frown deepened. "Kate, you're running on fumes."

"I'm fine."

"No, you're not." He dragged a hand through his hair, frustration evident. "You just watched a woman die."

A shiver ran down my spine. Watched. That wasn't exactly true. I hadn't just watched Isabella fall—I had fought her, struggled with her, and then she was gone. Disappearing into the abyss.

I shook my head, trying to push the memory aside. "You saw what I sent you, Liam. The documents. The fake identities. Isabella wasn't who she said she was."

His expression darkened. "Yeah, and now the cops are digging into it. If there's anything to find, they'll—"

A knock at the door interrupted him.

Liam and I exchanged a look before he moved toward it, peering through the peephole. With a sigh, he unlatched the lock.

Detective Harris stepped inside.

She was a woman in her forties, with sharp, calculating eyes that made it impossible to lie to her. Her dark blazer was dusted with rain, her expression unreadable.

"Mrs. Donovan," she greeted, then glanced at Liam. "Mr. Donovan."

Liam stiffened. "Did you find something?"

Harris let out a slow breath. "We searched Isabella's house."

I sat up straighter, my heart pounding. "And?"

She hesitated for half a second, then stepped forward, placing a plastic evidence bag on the coffee table. Inside was a small leather-bound journal, its pages yellowed with age. My stomach twisted.

"We found several of these," Harris continued. "Hidden in a locked compartment in her closet."

I leaned forward, my fingers itching to reach for it, but I held back. "What do they say?"

Harris met my gaze. "For starters, Steven never existed."

I exhaled sharply. Even though I had suspected it, hearing it confirmed made my skin crawl.

"She made him up?" Liam asked.

Harris nodded. "There's no record of a Steven Harrington. No marriage license, no past addresses, nothing. She built an entire life around a person who never existed."

I swallowed hard. "Then who was she?"

Harris hesitated again, then said, "We're still piecing that together, but…" She flipped open the journal inside the bag, revealing slanted, meticulous handwriting. "According to her own words, this isn't the first time she's done this."

I stared at her. "Done what?"

Harris' gaze was steady. "Changed her identity. Moved into a new neighborhood. Built a new life. And every time, there was a pattern."

A sick feeling curled in my stomach.

"She seduced men," Harris continued, flipping through more pages. "Sometimes married, sometimes not. And then, they'd disappear."

Silence filled the room.

Liam was the first to speak. "Disappear how?"

Harris looked at him. "We don't know yet. But we're cross-referencing missing persons cases from cities she previously lived in."

I shook my head, trying to process it. "So… you're saying Isabella was some kind of—what? A con artist?"

Harris didn't blink. "That would be the mildest way to put it."

A chill ran down my spine.

She wasn't just a liar. She wasn't just manipulative. She was dangerous.

"She's done this before," I whispered, more to myself than anyone else. "She's moved into neighborhoods, created these fake lives, lured people in, and then…" I trailed off, nausea rising in my throat.

Harris set the journal back down. "We'll know more once we analyze all the entries, but it's clear this wasn't just a one-time thing. And, Kate…" She hesitated, her voice lowering slightly. "One of the journals suggests she's lived in this neighborhood before. Under a different name."

My breath hitched.

"No," I said, shaking my head. "That's not possible. She—she just moved here."

Harris studied me. "Are you sure?"

I opened my mouth, but the words wouldn't come. Was I sure? I had never actually checked. We had all just… accepted that she was the new neighbor. That she and her husband had moved in a few months ago.

My stomach turned.

"She's been playing this game longer than we thought," Harris continued. "And you were the first one to see through her."

I let out a shaky breath.

"What happens now?" Liam asked.

"We keep digging," Harris said simply. "And we figure out exactly who Isabella Harrington really was."

Liam nodded, but I barely heard them. My mind was still stuck on one thing.

She had lived here before.

I had a sinking feeling that I knew what that meant.

This wasn't random.

She had come back for a reason.

***

I couldn't sleep.

Even after Harris left, after Liam had practically forced me to drink some tea and lie down on his couch, my mind wouldn't shut off. My body was exhausted, but my thoughts kept running in circles, pulling me into a loop of unease.

Isabella wasn't who she claimed to be.

Steven never existed.

She had lived here before.

And now she was dead.

I turned onto my side, staring at the faint glow of the streetlights filtering through the blinds. Every time I closed my eyes, I saw her face—not the polished, charming version of Isabella that had fooled everyone, but the version I'd seen in her final moments. Desperate. Enraged. Terrified.

Had she been afraid of me? Or was it something else?

I sat up with a frustrated sigh, rubbing my hands over my face. My phone sat on the coffee table, the screen dark.

I hesitated, then reached for it and scrolled to my messages.

The last text I had sent to Isabella was still there.

Kate: I know the truth. We need to talk.

I swallowed hard.

At the time, I had thought I was in control. That I had finally cornered her. But now, looking at it, I realized just how wrong I had been. She had been the one leading me. Manipulating the situation.

She had called me to the cliffs.

She had wanted me there.

But why?

A sharp knock at the door made me jump.

I turned, my heart hammering. Liam was in the kitchen, rummaging through a cabinet, but he must have heard it too because he shot me a questioning look.

"Expecting anyone?" he asked.

I shook my head, suddenly uneasy.

Liam moved toward the door and peered through the peephole. A second later, he muttered a curse and unlatched the lock.

Detective Harris stepped inside, her face grim.

"We found something," she said.

My stomach twisted. "What?"

She didn't answer right away. Instead, she pulled out her phone and swiped through something before holding it out to me.

I hesitated, then took it.

A photo filled the screen—an old driver's license. The woman in the picture looked… familiar. Same sharp cheekbones. Same dark, piercing eyes. But the name printed at the top wasn't Isabella Harrington.

It was Marie Calloway.

My breath caught.

"She was here before," Harris said, watching my reaction. "Over a decade ago. Different name, different life. But same face."

I looked up at her, my skin cold. "What happened to Marie Calloway?"

Harris' expression darkened. "She disappeared."

I felt like I couldn't breathe.

She disappeared?

Liam stepped closer, frowning. "What does that mean?"

"She vanished," Harris clarified. "One night, she just… left. No forwarding address. No goodbye. No trace. People assumed she moved. But considering what we know now—"

"She was running," I finished, my voice barely above a whisper.

Harris nodded. "And now she came back."

The weight of it settled deep in my chest. Isabella—Marie—hadn't just picked this neighborhood by chance. She had a reason for coming back. A reason for playing her game here, of all places.

I swallowed hard. "What else do you know?"

Harris hesitated before saying, "There's something else you should see."

She reached into her pocket and pulled out another evidence bag. This one held a small, yellowed photograph.

I took it with shaking hands.

It was a picture of a man. Tall. Smiling. His arm wrapped around a woman—Isabella. Only she looked younger. Less polished. But it was her.

I turned the photo over. Scribbled on the back in faded ink were the words: J & M – Forever.

J & M.

I looked up at Harris. "Who's J?"

"That's what we're trying to find out," she said. "But my guess? He was her original target."

I clenched my jaw. "And if he disappeared?"

Harris met my gaze. "Then we may have just found Isabella's first victim."

***

The rest of the night passed in a blur.

After Harris left, Liam insisted I stay close to him instead of being alone. I didn't argue. The idea of being by myself, surrounded by the remnants of this nightmare, was unbearable.

But sleep still didn't come.

The picture of Isabella—Marie—lingered in my mind, along with that mystery man. J.

Who was he?

What had happened to him?

And why had Isabella come back after all these years?

Sometime around dawn, I finally drifted into a restless sleep.

And that's when I saw her.

Not the Isabella I had known, but a different version. One with hollowed eyes and a cryptic smile, standing at the edge of the cliffs.

Her lips moved, but I couldn't hear the words.

And then, just like before, she fell.

I woke with a gasp, my chest heaving, sweat dampening my skin.

Liam was already awake, sitting at the kitchen table with his laptop open. He glanced up when he saw me stirring. "Morning."

I ran a hand through my hair, still shaken. "Any updates?"

He hesitated, then turned the screen toward me.

There, on the webpage, was a missing persons report.

Filed over ten years ago.

For a man named James Calloway.

J & M.

My stomach dropped.

He was her husband.

And he had vanished—just like all the others.

CHAPTER 8

TWISTED CONCLUSION

The days turned into weeks, and though the world outside moved on, the shadow of that night on the cliffs still clung to me. The police had searched tirelessly, sending divers into the churning waters below and scouring the rocky terrain. But Isabella's body was never found.

At first, they assured me it was just a matter of time. That the ocean would give her up, that the tides couldn't keep a secret forever. But as the weeks passed, their searches became less frequent, their updates more routine. Eventually, the investigation faded from the news, becoming just another unsolved mystery, buried beneath fresher headlines.

For a while, I couldn't sleep without seeing her face—the madness in her eyes as she lunged, the way the wind had swallowed her scream. And then the terrifying possibility that maybe she had survived. That she was out there somewhere, waiting and watching.

But I refused to let her steal anything more from me.

Liam was my anchor. He stayed by my side through every nightmare, every shuddering breath, every moment of doubt when I questioned whether it had really happened at all. And through it all, his love never wavered.

One evening, weeks later, I sat curled up on the couch, watching the golden hues of sunset stretch across the sky through our living room window. The scent of fresh coffee filled the air, mixing with the crisp scent of Liam's cologne as he stepped into the room.

He held out a steaming mug, sitting beside me as I wrapped my hands around the warmth. "You looked like you needed this," he said softly.

I smiled, leaning into him. "You always know."

His arm slipped around my shoulders, pulling me closer. "I just want you to feel like yourself again," he murmured, pressing a kiss against my temple.

"I do," I said, and for the first time, I actually meant it. "Because of you."

He cupped my face, his thumb tracing my cheek. "How about a trip?"

I blinked up at him. "A trip?"

"Yeah," he said, smiling. "Something just for us. No memories of cliffs, no cops, no past. Just you and me at my grandmother's place. It's quiet, peaceful. You'll love it."

A slow warmth spread through me, chasing away the last of the cold fear that had clung to me for weeks. "That sounds perfect."

His grin widened. "Good. Because I may or may not have already booked our tickets."

I laughed, shaking my head. "You're impossible."

"And you love me for it."

Liam always knew how to make things right, and I couldn't be more grateful for a partner like him.

***

A week later, we were packing.

Liam's grandmother's house was waiting for us—a quiet, tucked-away place with wide-open fields and fresh air, far from the memories lingering in this one.

I stood in the middle of our half-packed living room, taping up another box. "Are you really sure about this?" I asked, glancing at Liam.

He was stacking books into a crate, his movements calm, unrushed. "Moving for a while? Absolutely."

I sighed, smoothing a hand over the cardboard lid. "It just feels... sudden."

Liam came over and cupped my face, his thumbs tracing soft circles on my cheeks. "We need this, Kate. You need this."

I let out a shaky breath. "And what about you?"

His lips curved into a small smile. "I'll breathe easier knowing you're okay."

A lump formed in my throat. He always did this—always made me feel safe, even when my world had tilted completely off its axis.

"You're kind of perfect, you know that?" I murmured.

Liam chuckled, pressing a kiss to my forehead. "It's my job as your husband."

The word settled in my chest, warm and solid. My husband. My future. And for the first time in weeks, I let myself believe that maybe I was ready to move forward.

***

Liam's grandmother's house was nestled deep in the countryside, the kind of place where time slowed down, where the air smelled like pine and earth, and where the only sounds at night were the distant hum of crickets and the rustling of leaves in the breeze.

It was exactly what I needed.

Days passed in a blur of peace—slow mornings on the porch with steaming coffee and Bella sleeping next to me, barefoot walks through the dew-kissed grass and late nights wrapped in Liam's arms under a blanket of stars. For the first time in what felt like forever, I wasn't looking over my shoulder.

"See?" Liam murmured one evening, as we lay in a hammock strung between two old oak trees. "Told you this place would be good for us."

I tilted my head up, studying the easy smile on his face. "Yeah, yeah. You were right."

His fingers traced lazy patterns on my arm. "You know, you're cute when you admit that."

I laughed softly, swatting at him, my heart swelling at how easy everything felt again.

***

Weeks Later

The moving truck rumbled down the quiet road, tires crunching over gravel as it came to a slow stop in front of a charming white house a few doors down from Liam's grandmother's.

I watched from the porch, my fingers wrapped around a glass of iced tea, as a man stepped out first—tall, broad-shouldered, wearing a crisp button-down that looked too polished for a place like this. He stretched, rolling out the tension from the long drive, then turned to the passenger side.

She stepped out gracefully, her movements fluid, almost rehearsed. Her dark hair cascaded over her shoulders as she took in her new surroundings with an appreciative gaze.

"It's perfect," she murmured, trailing her fingers over the wooden fence, as if reacquainting herself with something long forgotten.

Something about her voice made my stomach twist.

A neighbor, an older woman from down the street, strolled over to welcome them, her small dog trotting at her feet.

"Well, hello there! You must be the new folks moving in. I'm Martha."

The woman turned, flashing a warm, inviting smile.

"It's so nice to meet you, Martha. I'm Sophie."

Her voice was kind and her smile was warm.

But a chill ran down my spine.

Because somewhere, deep in my bones, I knew that I'd heard that voice before. It was her.